HEAVEN'S GUN

AN EVE OF LIGHT SHORT STORY

HARAMBEE K. GREY-SUN

HYPERVERSE BOOKS, LLC

ALSO BY HARAMBEE K. GREY-SUN

Standalone Stories

Beholder

Love Among the Ultramoderns

The *EVE OF LIGHT* Series

The Novels

BloodLight: The Apocalypse of Robert Goldner (*Prequel*)

Broken Angels (*Book I*)

Divinities, Entangled (*Book II*)

The Short Stories

FoolKillers

The Lark

Heaven's Gun

Knotty & Ice

Rogue Beauty

Deviant-Hunter's Sabbath

BY HARAMBEE GREY-SUN

Poetry

Spring's Fall (Autumn Numbers * Book I)

Wine Songs, Vinegar Verses

This book is a work of fiction. Names, characters, places, and incidents are the products of the author's imagination or are used fictitiously. Any resemblance to actual events, locales, or persons, living or dead, is entirely coincidental.

Cover design by Adrijus G. from RockingBookCovers.com.

ISBN-13: 978-1-64044-904-6

Published by **HyperVerse Books, LLC**

www.hyperversebooks.com

writing between and beyond the lines

HEAVEN'S GUN

The signs had been taped to each door on the first floor. Some rabble-ramble about there being a smoker on the floor . . . smoking being against condo rules, which had the effect of law . . . smoke endangering children . . . cops being called next time smoke was detected . . . *blah blah bluh*.

Jacob couldn't be bothered to read all five paragraphs. It was three-thirty in the morning. He'd already put in fourteen hours today. When he saw the screed taped to his own door, though, he was tempted to put in a few extra minutes bothering someone else.

He didn't consider himself exempt from condo community rules, but it seemed he was being singled out. Only the sign on his door had words underlined in red.

Cigarette smoke permeated the hallway as it always did in the late hours. Whoever the smoker really was—Jacob honestly didn't know or care—the fiend had probably stayed up to the wee hours and turned in an hour or two ago. Probably a double-shift worker like himself.

Jacob ripped the leaflet down from his door with one

hand as he unlocked and turned the handle with the other. Sheila knew not to raise too much of a fuss at this hour. Like Jacob, she was a respectful tenant. But the bull terrier didn't hesitate to paw at his thighs while issuing whimpers almost as loud as barks.

"Sorry, girl." Jacob locked the door behind him. "You're on your own tonight." He knelt down to untie his Timberlands, trying to annoy rather than be annoyed by Sheila licking his hands and face. "Done all the walkin' I plan on doin' till I get some rest." He scratched her behind the ears as he stood. "C'mon."

He led Sheila to the patio door and opened it. The bull terrier looked out into the darkness, then back up at him. Jacob shook his head. Sheila again paused to look outside before reluctantly trotting out.

She'd roam, relieve herself, roam some more, then return when she was good and ready. She'd be gone for a minimum of ten minutes, a maximum of forty-five or so. She'd pick up the empty plastic bowl Jacob always left on the patio and tap it against the glass door—her secret knock —when she was ready to come in.

He was ready to relax. He turned on the stereo's CD player and pushed in a compilation of obscure blues singers singing slightly less obscure songs from the 1930s and 1940s. It was the only kind of music that could rub the knots out of his neck.

He leaned back in his recliner and closed his eyes, contemplating bourbon and sketching out the day ahead. He'd volunteered for the late-breakfast shift at the diner. It was a Friday, and late morning was the sweet spot—the time when a lot of the best paying customers began setting their plans for the evening. He had time for two, maybe two and a half hours of shut-eye before he needed to shower.

Someone banged on the front door, jolting him out of a reverie. He was expecting Sheila's tapping, or even barking. That he was used to. The pounding he'd heard instead gave birth to a minor headache.

He turned the music down on his way to the door, expecting a neighbor with a noise complaint. He looked out the peephole. One of two cops was staring back at him.

They weren't there to arrest him. He knew that protocol. The banging would've been fiercer and accompanied by the louder announcement and command: *Police! Open up!*

They could've been scammers. He knew that protocol as well. Crooks dressed up like cops, and when some unsuspecting chump opened the door, they'd beat and rob him.

He eyed his Glock on the bookshelf next to the door. He had strategically camouflaged and hidden it from casual observers behind a stack of books. Other guns were hidden around the apartment, including behind the stereo, but this was the closest. It was the easiest to reach if there were ever trouble on his doorstep.

It had been years since the possession of guns was made illegal for those outside law enforcement, but—at home or away—he always tried to keep one near his person. No need to have one in hand just yet, though. He was tired, but he was swift.

He cracked open the door. "Yes, officers?"

"We had a complaint."

"I turned the music down," Jacob said. "I'll keep it down."

"Not about that. About smoking."

"What?" Jacob's gaze shifted from one cop to the other. "I don't smoke."

"We had a complaint," the first cop said. "We have to follow up."

"Someone called building management," the second cop said, "and management called us. We agree some of these condo policies are a little silly, but in this state their rules have to be enforced by us."

"I *don't* smoke," Jacob said. "I can't afford to. I've already had one scare with my heart."

"Can we come in?"

Jacob didn't even glance at his bookshelf. He had enough close-up experience with cops—watching their movements, reading their badges, listening to their tone of voice—to know they were the real deal. If they'd seen him glancing, they would've become suspicious. No need to provoke them. Of course, they could've been corrupt cops, out to beat and rob him regardless. Most likely, he figured they were cops on the tail end of their late shift who had nothing better to do.

"Sure." Jacob stepped backward and opened the door wider. "Come on in." Normally he would've asked for a search warrant. But, again, no need to provoke.

The two men entered but didn't progress much beyond the doorway. Jacob kept his eyes on them as he made his way to the stereo. He turned it off but remained next to it, ready to grab the Glock behind it if necessary.

"Not much of a smell in here," the first cop said.

Jacob shook his head. "Only what you brought in with you."

The cops glared at him.

"And, me too," Jacob said. "The smoke is still on my clothes from when I got in a few minutes ago."

"Getting in from where?" the first cop asked.

"Work."

"Where do you work?"

"This an interrogation?" He'd humored them—they

knew he wasn't the villainous smoker—but now he was tired of them. If they were going to make some kind of move, he wanted them to get on with it.

"Just asking," the second cop said. "You look familiar."

Jacob smirked. "I work at the diner on Baker Street. Maybe you've eaten there."

The cop stared and then nodded, but said nothing.

"And I've got to be back at work in a few hours," Jacob said, "so if you don't mind."

The cops exchanged glances. The second cop turned and put his hand on the doorknob, then hesitated. It looked as if he were preparing to lock it.

Jacob took a step forward. On top of the stereo, his right hand inched toward the back edge, ready to snatch his piece. He could have it in hand, safety off, and pointed in less than two seconds.

The first cop wasn't looking at Jacob's hand. He seemed to be studying his face. Finally, he nodded and said, "Have a good night. Maybe we'll see you down at the diner soon."

They left without another word. Or glance.

Jacob locked the door behind them and looked out the peephole.

They were gone, or at least out of sight.

It didn't take long to figure who'd called them here in the first place: the Ethiopian, five doors down. Whoever the smoker was, Jacob was sure it was someone within two doors of that guy.

The Ethiopian . . . the same guy who'd refused to ever even nod "hello." The same guy who couldn't be bothered to hold the front door when Jacob's arms were burdened with groceries. The same guy with those three brats who ran up and down the halls when he was trying to nap. *He* was the one.

It took Jacob only a second or two longer to figure why the police had eyed him so. Did they know what he really did, or did they just catch his slip? The diner closed in the early evening and there was no way he could've just been getting home from work. Not unless he had another job.

He walked to the patio door and checked his watch. It was nearing four-thirty. Sheila should've been back already. Peering out, he saw nothing on the patio. Her tapping dish was untouched.

He'd entertained fears in the past. Letting Sheila run free, contrary to the city's leash laws, was just inviting someone to pick her up or poison her. But, even though she was his little sweetheart, Jacob knew no one could grab her without a fight, and she was too picky of an eater to be easily poisoned. No, she was a wily one. She'd taught Jacob a few tricks. The way his pre-dawn morning was turning out, however, he found it a little harder to push away dread.

He grabbed a jacket and flashlight, left two lamps on, then locked the patio door behind him. He knew Sheila's favorite and less traveled routes. He followed one of them at random while calling her name.

He entered the woods, treading a dirt path frequented by dog-walkers and joggers. It stretched on for miles, winding behind several housing complexes. He wasn't worried about waking anyone. The early risers were already waking, turning on their lights and radios and getting ready for work. Buses were beginning their routes, and garbage trucks would soon join them. One man calling a woman's name wouldn't bother anyone.

But Sheila didn't respond. Despite the flashlight, Jacob stumbled more than once, mixing curses with her name, which didn't help. It was ten minutes before he saw his little girl, pacing in front of a dense cluster of ferns and stopping every so often to issue a whimpering bark.

"Sheila? What is it?"

The bull terrier barked again but didn't even glance in his direction.

Jacob approached, looking around him. Beyond several rows of trees was a middle school. On the other side were three-story houses. Upper middle class territory.

Standing next to her, he asked again, "What is it, Sheila?"

She hunched down, pointing her nose. Jacob crouched. He used the flashlight and his free hand to untangle the weave of vegetation until he saw it. He blinked a few times and shook his head, something in him not wanting to believe he was staring at a gun.

It was black, the color of starless midnight, hard to really distinguish even with the flashlight shining on it. At first glance, it resembled a Colt Anaconda, but he knew it wasn't. It wasn't quite like any other revolver or even any other handgun he'd ever seen. Even on the current black market, where all kinds of firearms from the past hundred years could be found relatively easily, this thing would've been an oddity. He couldn't resist picking it up.

It was ice cold, but Jacob grasped instead of dropping it. He was surprised the handle warmed almost instantly and to such a degree that the warmth enveloped his hand. It was as if he'd put on a glove. He ran his left hand over the barrel. It didn't feel like metal; it was more like some kind of tough plastic, radiating warmth.

He heard two separate rustles in the treetops—one in the tree directly above him and one nearby. There was no breeze, and the commotion sounded like much more than what a squirrel could manage. Tiredness and confusion may have been feeding his paranoia, but he thought it best to move away quickly.

He tucked the gun into his jacket's holster. Worried over Sheila, he'd made the rare mistake of leaving his pad while unarmed. If there were someone in the woods who meant him harm, he wanted something in his possession.

He rationalized his taking the gun in retrospect when he was halfway home and realized he still had it. The initial grab had been done out of pure instinct, part of a basic will to survive. Sheila had kept up as he ran and, at the halfway point, took the lead.

He hustled after her. He hadn't heard any other noises behind him, but the right side of his chest, which was closest to the gun, felt warm. There was something special about the piece. He wanted to get home, safely, and examine it.

He checked behind him before he stepped onto his patio. Nothing.

He let Sheila inside, looked around again, then locked the patio door behind him. He pulled the blinds over the glass then headed toward the kitchen.

He laid the gun on the counter. He expected it to be glowing, but it remained black as obsidian. He stared at it for a moment, trying to figure the source of the warmth—as if sight alone would tell him—before he decided to open the cylinder. It'd be a good idea to check if the piece were loaded, and with what.

The gun was again ice cold but warmed instantly like before. An oddity, but it was nothing compared to what he saw when examining the cylinder. Each chamber appeared as if it were the inside of a tiny geode.

What the hell had he picked up?

His head jerked at the sound of a piercing screech coming from his bedroom.

The alarm clock. The alarm near his recliner would sound off in ten minutes. Jacob checked his watch. No hope of getting any decent shut-eye at this point. He decided he may as well head out to the diner early.

He carried the gun with him as he shut off the alarms. He then took it with him into the bathroom. Strange as the thing was, he wanted it near him. He allowed a significant distance only when he left it on the sink during the five minutes he spent in the shower. Even then, he did his best to keep an eye on it through the transparent shower curtain.

He dressed quickly then put out some food for Sheila. All the while, the bull terrier kept her eyes trained on the gun in her master's waistband. "Be back around four for dinner," he told her.

Thankfully, it was a crisp day. He could wear his work jacket over his regular outfit and no one would question it. Like many of his other jackets, it had a hidden holster that would cradle his new baby quite nicely. He usually didn't carry at work, just kept a piece in his car. But he wasn't going to part with his new foundling. Not until he knew more about it.

He set his apartment's alarm and walked out the front door. Down the hall, the Ethiopian was hustling his kids out of the apartment, no doubt preparing to escort them to the bus stop.

On any other morning, Jacob would've turned away and headed for the floor's other exit. Today, something impelled him to approach.

The Ethiopian seemed to notice him only after all the kids had been shuffled into the hall. After closing and locking his door, he turned to find Jacob almost nose-to-nose with him. Neither man moved.

"Call the cops on me again," Jacob said, "and I'll give you a damn good reason to."

Jacob turned and walked toward the farther exit. He restrained himself from shoving any of the kids out of his way. He tried to walk as straight a line as possible, hoping the Ethiopian would call his bluff. Instead, he heard the man nervously whispering to his kids, hurrying them toward the closest exit.

The left side of Jacob's chest felt warm. He smiled.

JACOB SCANNED THE CUSTOMERS, again, as he wiped the counter. From his first day on the job, he'd spent every free moment studying people—their faces, their clothes, their body language, their dietary preferences . . . everything he could think of. It helped him better serve his customers. He knew the regulars. He knew what they wanted to eat as soon as they stepped in the door based on the time of day and what they were wearing. At this point, he even had a good feel for strangers. He could guess what they might want just by the way they walked and their expressions. He was right fifty percent of the time.

Studying people and pegging them correctly served him well as an assistant manager in the restaurant business. The talent served him even better in a more lucrative side business.

Today, among sixteen regulars, he spotted four plain-clothes cops—one or two were possibly undercover, two were clearly detectives—and three cops sporting the shameful uniforms of beat walkers.

He knew one of the plainclothes and two of the men in uniform; he'd often chatted with them. In the guise of small talk—and while offering copious amounts of free coffee for the services they provide to the community—he learned as much as he could about their daily routine and that of their fellow officers without appearing suspicious.

Brennan, the diner's owner, had had several brilliant ideas. One was to create an establishment that served as a fast food joint for those on the go and an old-school diner experience for those eating in. Cops were generally drawn to the latter experience, whereas customers on the opposite side of the fence were drawn to the former. Another brilliant idea was to establish the joint just two blocks away from the police station. The place always had four or more cops as sit-down customers, and they were treated exceedingly well: free coffee and pastries and half off everything else. The badges were comfortable in here. Here, they let down their guard.

Jacob made eye contact with a man as he pushed through the left side entrance. Five o'clock shadow. Late thirties. Dark-wash jeans, sports jacket over a button-down . . . hip guy with a hip job taking an early lunch . . . because he could afford to take lunch whenever he wanted without being reprimanded. He made decent money. He was willing to spend money on indecencies. He was a Johnny-Mark. The two darting rightward movements of his eyes when Jacob made contact were as good as a secret handshake.

Jacob casually made his way to his register and signaled to all those waiting that it was open for business. The diner usually kept only one register open. The second was opened either when cops entered and signaled they were in a hurry or when the line at the first register was more than nine people long. The line had been twelve-people deep before Jacob stepped up.

The Johnny-Mark got in Jacob's line. When it became the Johnny-Mark's turn to order, Jacob clutched the side of the register with his left hand and curled the ring finger just so while letting the pinky stick straight out.

"Would you like to try the number six?" Jacob asked.

"I would like to try the number nine, *special*," the Johnny-Mark said.

"Chicken, beef, pork, or—"

"Beef."

"How would you like your eggs?"

"Over easy."

"Drink?"

"Coffee. With cream and sugar."

"Carry out, or—?"

"Dine in."

"Got it, chief," Jacob said with a nod. "Your number's on your receipt. Please step to the left."

The exchange could've gone any number of ways. There were many combinations Jacob and the customer could've used.

As the Johnny-Mark had given him the key terms, Jacob had pushed the appropriate buttons on the register. The folks in the back would prepare the customer's food, exactly as ordered, but on his tray, under a protective sheet, they'd include another sheet detailing the profiles of the type of girl he'd ordered for later that evening.

Special nine over six? The customer wanted *real* action. Beef over chicken or pork? He wanted his action figure to have curves where it counted, not model thin or big and beautiful. Eggs over easy? He wanted the girl to pamper him like a king, or a father. He didn't want scrambled—give-and-take rough sex—or fried—a girl who would essentially play dead while he did anything and everything short of actually killing her. Coffee with cream and sugar? He wanted an ethnic girl—but not too ethnic, preferably a mixed girl or someone who was at least light skinned. Dine in? In-call at a decent hotel rather than in-call at a cheap motel.

It was never too difficult to fit the specifications of a Johnny-Mark's desires—not as difficult as it should've been, considering Jacob's partners offered girls only under the age of eighteen. Jacob knew there were five or six girls who fit the profile of what this Johnny-Mark had specified. All of them would be on the sheet. After finishing his meal and leaving, the Johnny-Mark would review the profiles, make his choice, and then call the number on the sheet. Calls only. No text messages. The man who answered—one of Brennan's brothers—wanted to hear the voice of whomever he was speaking to. Certain telltale signs would result in him clicking off the phone, disposing of it, and calling the whole thing off. But the Johnny-Marks who weren't cut off gave the brother a series of three numbers—the same numbers on the receipt—that, when deciphered, gave three pieces of information: the proposed time of the appointment, the amount of time proposed for the appointment, and the base amount the Johnny-Marks were willing to spend, which was never under fifteen hundred. In turn, they received a series of numbers that, when deciphered, gave the time of the appointment, name of the location, and the number and time to call to get more details. Specifics would be nailed down during the second call.

It was a complicated code, but it had to be. Thanks to the law known euphemistically as the Mistress Act, anyone involved in a pay-to-play sexual activity was guaranteed a minimum three-year prison sentence. One strike and you were in. The multiple levels of screening served to protect the operation and its customers, and the customers were invariably the types who had or were willing acquire whatever funds necessary to enter the playground.

Jacob had already served time in jail for armed robbery and assault. He had no interest in serving time in the type of places they housed sex offenders. In holes like that, getting raped by a gang of fellow prisoners was the least of one's worries.

But he wasn't worried about anything today. The Johnny-Mark he'd just served had given off no weird vibes, nor had the two others who'd come in before him. Jacob watched as the guy nonchalantly ate his meal. The cops in the diner paid him no mind.

It'd been a very good day so far. His heart felt warm.

JACOB and his partners used only hotels or motels. Never residences, not even those located in less populated areas. It was far too risky.

Hotels and motels carried their own risks, but they were manageable. There were only ten that his partners would use. All the managers and relevant staff were paid off with drugs, girls, or money, usually a combination. And his partners thoroughly checked the premises at least one hour prior to an appointment. When Jacob was overseeing, he used his talents to size up everyone he saw, doing his best to detect any pigs in sheep's clothing.

Presently, he was overseeing his third appointment of the evening, the first one at a hotel.

His boys were already in position. One man was watching the parking lot. Another was pretending to read in the lobby. Men were in the stairwells, and one was posted in the elevator bank on the ground floor. All of them had guns and tablets. All of them were poised to ping him if they saw anyone suspicious. There was also a man in the room adjacent to the girl's. Jacob would join him soon.

He knocked the secret knock on the girl's door.

Desiree opened the door as far as the chain would allow and peeked through the crack.

"Let me in," Jacob said.

The girl vacantly gazed at him for more than a moment before closing the door. She unhooked the chain and slowly reopened the door, allowing Jacob just enough room to slide through.

She was wearing pink panties and a white lace camisole, one Jacob had little trouble seeing through in spite of the room's dim lighting.

"How do you feel?" he asked.

Her eyelids fought to stay apart as she nodded. Jacob could tell she'd just taken the Jelly Raptures. She should've swallowed them twenty minutes ago. Unlike many of the other fifteen-year-olds his partners managed, this one needed a little extra schooling.

All girls were instructed to take a combination of Raptures about thirty minutes prior to meeting a Johnny-Mark. It took roughly twenty-five minutes for the effects to kick in. The right combination of the colored beans—in this case, two yellows with red speckles, two red-and-blue striped, and one golden brown with a single ivory dot— would help make the girl more compliant, more sensual, while remaining cognizant enough to read the cues of the Johnny-Mark, knowing when to go slow and when to push for the release.

Desiree may have waited too long to pop the beans. Jacob couldn't afford for her to be sloppy tonight.

"Anything I need to know about?" he asked.

The girl shook her head like a content cat. He took that as her answer.

"You feelin' as you should?" he asked. "You know what you need to do?"

The girl stepped forward and put her hand on his elbow. "Jake . . . Big Jake . . . I need . . ."

"What?" he said. "More?" It was easy enough to get anyone hooked on the Raptures. After all, they looked and tasted like fancy jellybeans. Pretty, sweet, and thoroughly corrupting. Just as any good drug should be—or any good trick, for that matter. But allowing a trick to go beyond her limit, especially one who was still a child in body and mind, was just asking for trouble that couldn't be easily handled.

Still, promises had to be made all around for the man in charge of this appointment to get what he wanted. "You'll get more JRs after you give the JM his happy ending."

The girl shook her head. "No . . . need to . . . *want* . . . to go home . . ."

Jacob chuckled. "Honey, you get to travel forever. That's what everyone stuck at 'home' wants. That's why you left yours, remember? You set out for adventure. Now you're in Heaven. All the pure pleasure you can get. Don't forget that."

". . . so tired . . ."

He shook his head. "Not tonight, you're not."

The girl swayed as if she were about to fall on her face. Jacob put her hands in his.

"Desiree, listen. I won't let anything happen to you. You do your job and I'll do mine. You can sleep in a few hours."

His phone chirped. He pulled it out of his pocket and

looked at the text. One of his partners had messaged that the Johnny-Mark was on his way up the elevator. Jacob checked the time on his phone. It was ten till ten. No hope of stalling him, not without arousing suspicion and scaring him away. He could only hope the drugs punched in sooner than usual.

He squeezed Desiree's hands. "Perform well—get this jackass to cough up three grand—and I'll give you tomorrow off. The entire day. Okay?"

The girl's head dropped. A half-hearted nod. That'd have to do for his answer. Best thing for him to do now was just get the hell out of the way and let her do her job. She'd done it often enough. She knew how to play. Jacob led her toward the bed and positioned her like a lounging Lolita.

As he left the room, he heard the elevator opening down the hall. He retrieved his key card and ducked into the adjacent room just as he saw the Johnny-Mark rounding the corner.

The man in the room nodded. "Heard this guy's a first-timer."

Jacob walked to stand behind him and gazed at the laptop monitor. "Everyone has a first time. Desiree's good. She'll have him beggin' to come back."

Both men watched the monitor. Two strategically placed cameras and three equally camouflaged microphones in Desiree's room ensured them a relatively complete picture of anything that happened in the room. The laptop could adjust the picture to compensate for the dim lighting. If the Johnny-Mark got out of hand, they'd see or hear and be on him in less than a minute. Jacob had brought two guns. The mystery one remained close to his heart, in his jacket's holster. His loaded Glock was tucked in his waistband at the small of his back. He hoped to keep it there. He and his partners wanted a long, uninterrupted performance that they could post online later.

The Johnny-Mark knocked the customer's knock on Desiree's door. She rose languidly from the bed and seemed to slide into character as she moved easily toward the door. It was too dark to read her facial expression, but the tone of voice seemed right as she said, "Coming."

After cracking the door to peep through, she let the man in. Dim light notwithstanding, there was no mistaking his smile. He was dressed all in black, with a jacket Jacob thought a little too heavy for the weather. Oh, well—the Johnny-Marks all had their little quirks. Jacob was more concerned with what he was carrying that with what he was wearing.

Along with the all-important greeting card, Johnny-Marks often brought flowers or candy to their hosts. The kinkier ones brought toys. This one could've brought any of the above; the greeting card was taped to a container the size of a shoebox. First-timers were usually so nervous they tended to overcompensate.

"Switch to split-screen mode," Jacob said. "We don't want to miss anything."

"What the hell'd he bring her?" his partner asked as he switched the view. "A chocolate bunny?"

Desiree put one hand on the man's shoulder and another on the strap of her camisole as she kissed him on the cheek. He turned away to place the box on top of the dresser.

"Is that for me?" Desiree sultrily asked.

The Johnny-Mark turned toward her. "Mind if I get more comfortable?"

"Of course not, baby," Desiree purred. "Need some

help?" She stepped forward and laid her hands on his jacket collar. He stepped back while removing her hands.

"I need to use the bathroom first . . . Maybe you want to join me? I may need an extra hand."

"Great," Jacob's partner said. "Another water-sports freak. He indicate that this morning?"

"No," Jacob said. "And he ain't gettin' it tonight."

Desiree giggled then raised her index finger in front of her face; she wagged it as she sexily shook her head. *Good girl*, Jacob thought. No matter what was asked, a girl always had to decline in a way that wouldn't upset the Johnny-Mark. The goal, after all, was always to squeeze as much money out of them as possible. Angry men didn't like to spend a lot of money. Jacob was happy the Raptures hadn't affected Desiree's memory. She knew what the man had ordered and what he hadn't. Jacob and the other handlers always took special care to coach his girls prior to their appointments.

The man closed the bathroom door behind him—all the way. Jacob furrowed his brow. This guy was giving off some funny vibes, far different from what he picked up as he took the guy's order that morning. The Johnny-Mark didn't appear nervous; it was something else. He hadn't kissed or even hugged the girl. Nor did he remove his jacket after he entered the room. What kind of Johnny-Mark wore his jacket into the bathroom?

Desiree glanced at the bathroom door then hurried over to the dresser. She pulled the envelope off the box, opened it, and peered inside. A pained expression spread across her face.

"What—?" Jacob's partner began.

Jacob tensed.

Desiree plucked out the greeting card, opened it, cursed,

and tossed it to the floor. She then peered inside the envelope again, cursed again, and ripped it in half. Both the card and the envelope had been empty.

Jacob saw the look on her face and wished he could shout through the wall—*Stay cool, girl. He may have all the money on him, or it may be in the box.*

Most Johnny-Marks laid the base amount—tucked in a greeting card—on the table when entering; they kept the tip —usually sizable—on their person. The break in protocol seemed to confuse her. Staying cool was the thing Desiree was least prepared to do.

The bathroom door opened. The man was still fully clothed, jacket and all. Desiree turned toward him and shouted, "Where the fuck is the money?" The purr had become a growl.

"What?"

She started toward him. "I asked about the money, asshole! Where the fuck is it?"

A fail on two counts. The girl had obviously taken the wrong combination of Raptures, and perhaps too many. She was far angrier than she should've been, far angrier than Jacob had ever seen her. Not to mention careless. She knew she was to never mention money during an appointment.

"Money for what?" the man asked.

"No, Desiree, don't—" Jacob muttered as he took another step backward. He realized what was happening a moment before she said it.

"Did you want me to fuck you or not?" Desiree hollered. "Cuz you ain't gettin' shit without my money!"

"What?" the man said. "You mean you want money for sex? With that body?"

The girl lunged at him. The man sidestepped, palmed her face, and shoved her toward the bed. Desiree got up as quickly as she went down and rushed at him again. The man's hand went into his jacket and pulled out a taser. Desiree probably wouldn't have stopped even if she were fully aware of what was happening. The man shot her in the stomach without a word. Desiree's screaming said enough for the both of them.

It had all happened so quickly. Jacob had started toward the door as soon as the man said "sex." But the action on the screen played out in less than twenty seconds.

"All gone to hell," he said as he rushed out into the hall. He paused before he reached Desiree's door.

Two menacing figures were at the far end of the hall to his left. He turned. Two more figures, similarly outfitted, were down the hall to his right. They were covered in black from head to toe—from *helmet* to *boot*—and carrying semi-automatic pistols.

There was no trace of skin, no exposed areas on any of them. Nevertheless, he reached his right hand behind him.

"*Freeze!*" They all pointed their weapons at him. "Heart-land Security! *Don't* move!"

Jacob froze. His mind boiled. This whole damn thing was a setup. The man in Desiree's room was either a Heart-land Security agent or some kind of informant working with them. And he was well trained; Jacob hadn't detected even a hint of pig or rat in the diner. His boys downstairs hadn't warned him because they were either already subdued or they had been in on it from the beginning. And, of course, the jack-booted thugs had the means to convince the hotel staff to participate . . . Heartland Security—*not* cops. The Heartland Security Agency took the Mistress Act more seri-ously than local authorities, but surely they had more important things to do than come down on Jacob and his crew.

He held his position as the agents on either end steadily approached. In front of him, Desiree's door opened. The undercover stood in the doorway, holding the box he'd brought with him in both hands. Now in better light, Jacob saw it was neither a box of candy nor a box containing a toy. It wasn't even cardboard. It was metal plated. It was a container for something serious.

The man smirked at Jacob. "You know, we're not some bumfuck cops. We've known about your shitty little code for months. Deciphered the whole damn thing in less than a week. We know exactly what you and your pals have been doing."

Jacob was puzzled. He was careful not to make any sudden moves, but he noticed the agents on either end were still approaching very deliberately. The man in the doorway wasn't moving closer. It was almost as if they were afraid of Jacob.

Though they'd said nothing about it, he knew about his right to remain silent—but curiosity overwhelmed him. "Why didn't you ever take us down before?"

"You're small fish," the man said. "We only go after the big ones."

That meant they were after Brennan, the man at the top of the entire organization. He and his brothers had been involved with prostitution, drugs, and gun running long before they ever even set up shop in the area. Though Jacob had climbed a few steps in the organization, he'd never been part of the innermost circle. But—his thoughts still churning—he figured something had happened recently that had made him into something of a shark.

The agents on either side of him were no more than fifteen feet away. Not only his mind but his chest was burning. He couldn't remain still.

He rushed the man in the doorway. The man was taken off guard and, his hands full, easily taken to the ground. Jacob rolled off of him, slammed the door shut, and drew his Glock.

The man scrambled to get to his feet as he reached inside his jacket.

"Freeze," Jacob growled. "I see your hand come out, I pull the fuckin' trigger."

The man kept his hand where it was as he straightened. "They're going to come through that door any second, you know. They have a key card. You can't get out of this."

"What do you want?" Jacob asked.

"Lay your weapon down and we'll go easy on you. I promise."

Jacob glanced at Desiree. She wasn't moving. It appeared she wasn't even breathing. "You didn't go easy on her."

"What do you care?" The man seemed less frightened, more indignant now. "She's a child that you pimped out for sex. Just a sex slave you and your crew were holding prisoner."

"You didn't give a damn about her. Look at what *you* did. Treatin' her as a means to an end. You tell me what the end is."

The agent said nothing. Jacob wondered if his partner in the next room were sitting there listening, recording all this. Not that it mattered. The agents had seen Jacob come out of that room. They'd rush it and take down his partner soon enough. Fuck him, anyway.

"I'm no good guy," Jacob said, "but neither are you. I want to know exactly what you want from me, then I'll decide whether it's worth my time to cooperate."

There was a banging on the door. "You're out of time,"

the man said as he jerked his hand out of his jacket and aimed.

Jacob fired, plugging the man in the forehead.

The agents outside burst into the room.

Jacob turned and fired while scrambling for cover behind the bed, behind Desiree's body.

The agents' body armor withstood all bullets. Three of them took aim. Jacob ducked before they fired.

The bed was high enough off the ground for him to slide under. He could think of no other out.

He gained a few seconds, but now he was trapped. Done for. His Glock had one bullet left, and it wouldn't do him any good. These guys were armored up tight. His armor was nothing but khakis, t-shirt, and a jacket.

His chest throbbed. His heart was burning . . . The *gun*. That's what they were after.

But he couldn't get to it. No way now to pull it out and see what was so special about the damned thing. No—he had just one play left.

"I give up!" He shouted it until he heard the only words he wanted to hear.

"Come out slowly! To your left! Keep your hands empty and keep them visible at all times!"

"Coming!" he shouted back. "I'm leaving the Glock here under the bed! Don't shoot! I'm coming peacefully!"

Jacob laid the Glock on the floor to his right and edged his body toward the left.

"Keep your hands where we can see them!"

His widespread left hand was the first thing he slid out from under the bed. One of the agents grabbed it and pulled, dragging the rest of him out.

Jacob lay flat on his back, exposed, staring up at the

three firearms pointed at him. The fourth agent stood at his head. His gun was holstered.

"Backup is on the way," the fourth agent said. "We should just shoot you. You killed one of our agents. All of your people in this building are either dead or in custody."

Jacob almost said out loud, *Then why don't you just kill me?* It'd be a far better fate than an HSA-run prison.

"But we're still willing to give you a break. One last chance. Keep your hands where we can see them and stand up slowly."

He did as asked, though he didn't trust for one second they were going to give him a break.

The four surrounded him, one agent on either side, one in front, and one behind.

"You took something earlier today," said the agent to his right, the one who'd holstered his weapon. "Something that you found in the woods. I am asking you to hand it over."

"If you knew what I had, why didn't you pull me at the diner?"

The agent laughed. "Well, if we were going to move on you, we figured we might as well move on your little operation as well."

Yeah, if they took him down in the restaurant, Brennan and his brothers had several protocols in place to minimize damage to the rest of the organization. If the feds had known about Brennan for months, they had probably been waiting for the right time to move and shut down the whole thing. This wasn't that time, but they couldn't wait any longer. Or, at least, *these* feds couldn't. Jacob hadn't seen a single badge. He'd no doubt that they were HSA, but this was a dark unit. They'd moved tonight to take out a few pushers and pimps simply as cover, for public consumption. They were really here for just one purpose.

"If I hand it over?" Jacob asked.

"As I said, we'll give you a break."

Jacob had never dealt with HSA agents before, but he'd had enough experience with law enforcement to know how to read between the lines. The only break these assholes would give him would be between the shoulders and skull. They knew he had their gun—why didn't they just cuff him, frisk him, and *take* it?

He had an advantage. They knew it. And, now, so did he.

"It's inside my jacket," Jacob said. "It's not loaded. I'll take it out and throw it on the bed."

"No," the agent to his left said. "You'll take it out and place it in the box—*slowly*."

The agent to his right backed up and picked the rectangular box off the floor. He opened it and approached. Jacob looked inside.

It *was* a containment box—specifically for the gun. These hardened agents, even with their gloves and armor, were afraid to touch the weapon.

He wasn't.

He slowly brought his right hand down. "Takin' it out now. Just ease up, alright?"

Far as he could tell, each agent took exactly one step back—no more—as he reached inside his jacket. He wondered if any of these goons had been in the diner this morning. Had he served any of them breakfast? If so, he wondered what they'd eaten. If only he could see their faces . . . *Uptight assholes.* Constipated types like them should be eating oatmeal.

His fingers grasped the handle. It not only felt as if he'd slipped on a glove. It felt as if the glove were alive, and intelligent.

The agent behind him said, "Slowly . . ."

Jacob whipped the gun out and fired at the first helmet he saw and spun and fired at the next and the next. He only paused when aiming at the fourth agent, the one holding the box. For a moment, Jacob thought he could see through the black face shield; he thought he saw the expression of stark terror one second before he pulled the trigger. He stood watching as the face shield shattered, as if in slow motion, revealing a face spurting and gushing a lumpy gray liquid out of the nostrils, ears, and eyes.

Horrified and fascinated at once, Jacob remained rooted, gaping as the agent slumped and fell backward, the lumpy liquid continuing to spill as its pace eased from gush to ooze.

He weighed the gun in his hand. He didn't look at it. He was afraid to, briefly entertaining the notion that if he did, it might do something horrible to his face, to his *head*.

He turned his attention to the other agents. They'd met the same fate as their fallen partner—helmets shattered open, heads leaking gratuitous amounts of brain matter, matter that had been reduced to *oatmeal*.

The gun. The gun loaded with what-in-God's-name did this.

He heard distant voices coming from the hall. More agents were on the way. He had to move.

He cast an eye at the open containment box and considered carrying it with him. But what the hell for?

Have gun, will travel.

He ran out of the room. Pairs of agents were on either end of the hall. They must've been coming up the stairwells.

"Freeze!"

"Drop your weapon!"

"Don't move!"

Scramble 'em. Jacob didn't take much thought to aim. He

just pointed, fired, spun, and repeated. Each targeted body, when hit, exploded in a mess of blood, bones, and armor.

He'd gotten them all before any of them could get off a shot. But he wasn't one to wait around and admire his work. He turned to his right and bolted for the stairwell.

He pushed through the door and paused, his weapon ready. The stairwell was free of agents, but he had to descend ten flights before hitting fresh air. He could be ambushed at any second.

To hell with 'em all. To hell with their numbers, their armor, and their authority. He had the advantage. He had a gun that was a gift directly from *Heaven*.

He hustled down the stairs, hopping down two or three at a time when he could. He was approaching the seventh floor when the door opened. Someone was entering the stairwell.

A man, in plain clothes. Jacob couldn't tell if he was just a man or an agent. And he certainly couldn't wait for the man to pull a weapon.

Jacob aimed his gun and pulled the trigger. The man's head exploded in a fine red and yellow mist. Jacob leapt over the headless fool and tried to quicken his pace.

He made it to the bottom of the stairwell without further interruption, but he halted before pushing through the exit door.

The parking lot would be crawling with agents. He wasn't wearing any kind of armor. He wasn't invulnerable. One fool just had to get off one lucky shot and it'd be all over for him. He had to play this smart.

The agents upstairs hadn't shot him because they either wouldn't or couldn't touch the gun. He hoped the same trick would work twice.

He pushed through the door. Bright spotlights switched

on directly in front of him, blinding him. He raised his left arm over his eyes.

"Freeze!"

"Don't move!"

"Lower your arm!"

He slowly lowered his arm and was careful not to make any sudden moves. He was forced to squint in the face of the too-bright lights. He couldn't see how many agents there were. He couldn't see *where* they were.

"Slowly place your weapon on the ground—now!"

No. The gun belonged to him. It was a *part* of him. He felt it in his very heart, deep in his soul. But a thought struck. An idea. He hoped it was more than a whim. He prayed his new sense was leading him down the right path.

He slowly stooped and laid the gun on the ground.

"Lock your hands behind your head and kick the gun away from you!"

He did as instructed.

"Now get on your knees!"

He again followed orders.

"Don't move!"

He didn't. And, though still squinting, he finally saw agents entering his view. A few to the left, a few to the right, and some behind. None of them were his immediate concern. His main attention was on those approaching from the front. He didn't try to count how many. He was just waiting for enough of them to cross the paths of the spotlights, allowing him to see.

There.

He opened his eyes wide and focused on the gun, still lying on the ground. He concentrated. It shook. He sent it a thought. It began sliding in his direction.

Several agents noticed and shouted. Several more rushed forward.

Jacob *shoved* a thought at the gun. It hurtled itself toward him.

Jacob grabbed the gun, ducked, rolled, and came up to a knee, firing at every moving thing that crossed his field of vision. When it felt right, he rolled again, shifted position, and fired again.

The shouting shifted to screaming as agents exploded, collapsed in upon themselves, or experienced some other fatal torture. Blood flowed like milk or eased like syrup as some of the closer agents were riddled—puffed and flattened at once—like waffles.

Jacob hustled to his feet, running and shooting, as he made for the nearest cluster of parked cars. When he managed to hunker down between two vehicles, he heard two voices: the only two agents left alive. One screamed at the other to call for backup. The other shouted that they should just lay down heavy fire and put Jacob down.

He couldn't let them do either.

He'd gotten this far because no one wanted to touch the gun, and, once he began firing, the other agents were too shocked and awed at the results to effectively counterattack. These two remaining had gotten over their surprise. They'd kill him and figure out the rest later.

He'd have to regain the element of surprise.

He flattened himself on the ground and looked under the car toward the voices. One agent was approaching. Jacob wasn't sure where the other one was. Didn't matter. He had the general position of one. He just had to draw his attention.

He turned to his side and pointed the gun straight in the

air. He pulled the trigger. Several hundred feet up, a flare exploded.

Jacob stood, aimed over the car's hood at the confounded agent, and pulled the trigger.

It was as if a cannonball traveling at light speed had hurtled through the agent's midsection. He looked like a human-shaped donut as he teetered before falling to the ground.

I'll reduce the other one to hash, Jacob thought. But the other agent wasn't in view. Jacob didn't hear anything, either.

To hell with it. The other one probably ran away with wet pants. Jacob certainly wasn't going to chase him down. He instead hustled toward his SUV. He needed to get home and do a little thinking before making his next move.

As he neared the vehicle, he slowed his pace and checked out his surroundings.

Nothing.

No one.

The HSA must have cleared the lot before he arrived and ordered everyone to stay inside the hotel till they gave the all clear. That signal was going to come long after Jacob had left.

He unlocked his vehicle and settled himself inside. He started it up and laid the gun on the front passenger's seat. He checked all windows and mirrors before shifting into drive.

That last agent really must have run away. Jacob was free and clear. Even when he hit the road and exceeded the speed limit by twenty, he didn't see any flashing lights in the rearview.

But they'd come. They weren't just going to let him walk away with this—this gun from Heaven. Their second wave would be superior to the first. He'd have to be ready. He'd have to try to truly *understand* the gun.

Hell, what was there to understand? He pointed the gun, pulled the trigger, and it transformed his thoughts— subconscious if not conscious—into results. His aim didn't even have to be spot on, just close enough.

He could really go places with this. But he had to deal with the present before plotting a future.

He parked the SUV in his complex's lot. He placed Heaven's piece in his jacket and got out of the vehicle. He pushed the button on his keychain to lock it, then he smelled something.

Smoke. It was coming from him.

He checked the inside of his jacket. It wasn't burning, not even warm. But the smoke was coming from the gun. It didn't smell like gun smoke. It smelled more like incense. Jacob couldn't pin down the exact scent, but it grew heavier, thicker, as he made his way to the side entrance of the building. He was almost suffocating in the aroma as he walked the hall toward his front door.

Sheila was waiting for him as always when he entered, but she kept her distance, issuing only one bark when Jacob stepped inside.

"You need a walk," Jacob said, "and so do I."

He headed straight for the patio door. Sheila bolted out when he opened it. He didn't run after her. After locking the door behind him, he followed her route, but at his own pace.

His heart was as warm as usual when the gun was close to his chest. Beyond that, he and his jacket weren't affected by the gun's change. It was probably just an effect of him overusing it in one night.

At least the incense had more room to disperse in the

outside air. It bothered him less as he looked up at the stars, shut his eyes, and took a deep breath. The exhalation came out as a hoarse chuckle.

Brennan would want answers about how the night could have gone so wrong. That punk bitch would have bigger problems when Jacob saw him. Jacob wanted his whole operation. Guns, tricks, porn, drugs—hell, he'd even expand into gambling. Why not? He knew codes. He had imagination. He could certainly do better than those crooks operating in Atlantic City or Vegas. Shit, with his mind and this weapon from Heaven, he'd be running the entire region's underworld in no time. *Overlord of the underworld . . .* He chuckled again, louder.

"Must be some joke," he heard someone say.

"Care to share?" he heard a different voice say.

Jacob whirled around but saw no one. "Who—?"

Someone punched him in the face, a rapid right and left cross battered his cheeks, causing him to stumble backward and trip over a crouching body he couldn't see.

He cursed in pain and surprise on the way down. He managed to get up on a knee before he felt a boot kick him under his chin, forcing him down again.

HSA agents. Had to be. They were in some kind of armor that made them invisible.

Jacob stayed on his back as he reached for his piece. Someone stomped on his stomach. He hollered, balled up, and rolled to his side.

There were apparently two of them. One of them kicked him in the head and back while the other one spoke.

"We'd have preferred not to get involved. We usually just locate missing kids and lead the professional cleaners to the scum. We like to step back and let them do their job. But it looks like you found a toy. Guess we're force to play with you till the big guns arrive."

The voice wasn't a mature one. Sounded like a girl in her late teens or early twenties.

"Bitch," Jacob said, "I've got your big gun right here." He turned toward the one who was kicking him and thrust his whole body upward and forward. It seemed to surprise and knock the agent off balance, long enough for Jacob to draw his gun.

He pointed it toward the general direction of where he'd heard the voice and prepared to pull the trigger. The right side of his face exploded in searing pain, as if someone had hit him with a flaming bat.

He dropped the gun. Someone got him in a choke hold from behind. Jacob's knees buckled, allowing his attacker to tighten his hold even more. He could tell by the strength and aggressiveness exhibited that it was a male, but a young one.

Jacob used both arms to try to pry himself loose.

"You're not dealing with mere mortals anymore," the girl's voice said. "We can do things the likes of you couldn't possibly understand. Give up *now*."

He was more than tired of people telling him to lie down, stay put, and give up. He wasn't some bitch.

He kept his left hand on his assailant's arm while he stretched his right toward his gun. He tried to will it toward him.

Sheila shot out from nowhere, leaping and latching onto the invisible girl, who became visible when struck. All growl and tenacity, the bull terrier had gotten her by the throat. The girl flailed, trying at once to get the dog off and scramble away. But the bull terrier held on for dear life as it choke-bit out another's.

Jacob felt the choke hold loosen. He elbowed the guy behind him to get freer then reached out for his gun. In a second, it was in his hand. In another second, he whirled around and pulled the trigger.

He pegged it right. He pegged *him* right.

The kid flashed into sight when hit and immediately swelled up. He momentarily resembled a balloon figure made by a mad clown. And, when he popped, scattering his innards, Jacob laughed a hearty chuckle, even as a good portion landed on him.

He turned around to see Sheila still gnawing on the girl, who'd already begun a new existence as a corpse.

"Not mere mortals, huh?" he muttered. Yeah, they had a few tricks, but they looked and sounded like college students. Whatever they were, they hadn't a chance. His new appendage put him on equal footing with anything or anyone this planet shoved at him. *God's gun*—and he was the chosen one to wield it.

It now gave off a thicker smoke, a heavier scent, one that didn't disperse so easily. It lingered about him like a fog. But the piece still felt good in his hand. Like it never wanted to be released.

"Come at me, world!" he shouted. "I'm ready!"

Sheila burst into flames—flames that immediately snuffed out to leave a charred skeleton in their place.

Jacob froze.

"Sheila—?"

His little girl.

"*Sheila!*"

His body trembled uncontrollably.

"You said you were ready," a booming voice above him said. "I took you at your word."

Jacob looked up. Hovering several dozen feet in the air

was a creature at least ten feet tall, if not more. Appearing mostly as a man, it was nude. Its body had a bodybuilder's physique. Its head was a unicorn's. Its hands appeared to be talons; its feet were cloven hooves. From the neck down, all of him—all of *it*—was clothed in rippled folds of multihued but transparent light.

"What the hell—?" Jacob whispered.

The creature slowly descended.

Jacob pointed the gun and pulled the trigger.

The creature continued its descent.

Jacob again pulled the trigger.

The creature was no more than ten feet from the ground.

Jacob concentrated now—on exploding bodies, scrambled entrails, broken limbs, ruptured organs—and pulled the trigger at each thought.

The creature stood in front of him and gazed down into his eyes.

"I believe you are finished," the creature thundered.

Jacob's knees buckled. But he refused to go down. He wouldn't cower.

"The fuck are you?" he asked.

"I am the Equinox. The magick you are wielding will not work on me. It has been born of an inferior art form."

Jacob didn't understand any of it. He only knew his little girl was dead, and his newest protector wasn't working in his time of greatest need.

His shoulders heaved as the corners of his eyes welled up. His voice cracked and wavered. "It's over, isn't it?"

"For you. Your world. Your kind. And your ideas." The creature stretched its right talon forward. The gun flew to it and hovered over as the creature moved its left talon on top of it. The gun crumpled in upon itself until pea sized, then winked out of sight.

Jacob looked up into those frightening, equine eyes. They were ablaze with a blue fury. The sight was dreadful enough, but Jacob wouldn't turn away. He wouldn't bend to his knees or beg. He fought back his tears. He swallowed until he was sure he'd sound like a man, not a coward. "What now? What are you going to do to me?"

"You?" the creature thundered. "I do not give a damn about you."

The folds of faint light enveloping the creature ruffled furiously until they appeared as a dozen pairs of far-reaching wings. Like a crossbow's bolt, the creature shot straight into the air and was out of sight—all in the time it took Jacob to gasp.

It wasn't wholly an expression of awe. His gasp unleashed the floodgates holding back what he'd felt for Sheila. He dropped to his knees.

His world . . . In one night, he'd experienced such power, had such dreams, and then . . .

No. Mourning would have to come later. He needed rest. He needed to figure out how to deal with Brennan.

It took more than one try, but he pushed himself up to his feet. His eyes welled at another glance at Sheila's remains. He then turned, took a deep breath, and trudged home. He'd return to bury her when he was stable enough to pay the proper respects.

Half a mile later, his patio in sight, he still had no idea of what to do or where to go when the sun rose. He couldn't return to the diner. Hell, even spending the night at his own pad was tempting fate. Maybe he'd hit the road, drive south.

He stepped onto the patio and looked down. Sheila's plastic bowl was full.

He stooped and looked closer. Hamburger, partially cooked but mostly pink. It being there was strange enough, but something else was funny with it.

He dipped two fingers in and brought them up to his nose. Two whiffs were all it took. Some kind of chemical —*poison*—had been mixed in. But not too much. Sheila's sense of smell would've picked it up, but she may have chowed down, ingesting everything before realizing it could do her harm. That was the probably the hope, anyway, of whoever put this here.

Jacob stood, wondering who possibly could have—

The blade penetrated several inches deep in his neck. It slid out like a finger from a glove before thrusting in and sliding out of another part of his neck.

With no words and hardly a thought, Jacob fell to the concrete, landing on his side. A hand grasped his shoulder and turned him to his back as the blade plunged into his chest.

The man on top of him moved erratically, and Jacob was fading out quickly. But through squinting eyes and blurred vision, he recognized the Ethiopian, mad as all hell, stabbing his chest and neck with a rarefied fury. He wouldn't stop anytime soon.

Jacob couldn't fight back. He only tried to chuckle at his final thought—that he'd soon resemble the meat in Sheila's bowl.

ABOUT THE SERIES

Eve of Light is a Dark Metaphysical Fantasy series chronicling the surreal events leading up to the Apocalypse—the Death of God. The setting is a contemporary, alternate Earth on the verge of a cataclysm that will warp space, time, and minds. The main narrative of those plotting and battling to save humanity is told in the *Eve of Light* series of novels. The short stories and novellas are simply flashes on the fringe—episodes told from the perspective of everyday men and women living in a world turned weird.

The Core Novels

BloodLight: The Apocalypse of Robert Goldner
Broken Angels *(Eve of Light * Book I)*
Divinities, Entangled *(Eve of Light * Book II)*

Stories on the Fringe

FoolKillers
The Lark
Heaven's Gun
Knotty & Ice
Rogue Beauty
Deviant-Hunter's Sabbath

ABOUT THE AUTHOR

Harambee K. Grey-Sun writes under the broad umbrella of speculative fiction. He integrates elements of fantasy, horror, noir, black humor, and science fiction into his work and spins dark, surreal, mysterious, grotesque, at times challenging, and often blasphemous tales. Many of his stories can be categorized into one or more of the following subgenres: speculative thriller, urban fantasy, metaphysical fantasy, superhero, occult/supernatural, slipstream, and–*of course*– weird fiction. His Dark Metaphysical Fantasy series *Eve of Light* examines the dark nature of God and what it really means to be human.

For more information:
www.harambeegreysun.com